Krystal Ball is published by Picture Window Books,
a Capstone imprint
1710 Roe Crest Drive
North Mankato, Minnesota 56003
www.capstoneyoungreaders.com

Cataloging-in-Publication Data is available on the
Library of Congress website.
ISBN: 978-1-4795-2178-4 (library hardcover)
ISBN: 978-1-4795-3152-3 (paperback)

Summary: Krystal Ball is hoping for a dream
birthday, but her fortune-telling talents are
giving her nightmares.

Designer: Kay Fraser

Printed in China.
092013   007738LEOS14

stal Ball

DReam BiRthday

by Ruby Ann Phillips
illustrated by Sernur Isik

PICTURE WINDOW BOOKS

Table of Contents

My Future Awaits

Hi there! My name is Krystal Ball. I'm from Queens, which is a part of New York City. Some people call this place the Big Apple. But I live in a tiny, two-bedroom apartment with my mom and dad, so it seems pretty small to me.

Don't get me wrong...I love, LOVE my parents. My mom works as a hair stylist on the first floor of our building. My dad's a high school history teacher. He's always saying things like, "History repeats itself, sweetie." Whatever that means.

I'm not that interested in the past, though. I'm much more excited about...the future.

I like astrology, palm reading, and stargazing. Why? Well, let me tell you a little secret. I'm not exactly normal. I may look small, you see, but I'm really a medium. That means I have a special ability, kind of like a sixth sense. My grandma calls this my "gift". It helps me see what the future holds, but it's never quite clear. I can learn things about a person or an object by touching them and, sometimes, my dreams show little glimpses of events that haven't happened yet.

I usually have trouble understanding these visions, or premonitions, but I'm working on improving my skills. I also go to Nikola Tesla Elementary School, and being a fourth-grade fortune-teller while juggling science projects, math tests, and homework isn't easy.

What else can I tell you about me? Ah! My best friend, Billy, lives in the apartment above ours. I've known him my whole life, and that's a really long time. Almost ten years...Whoa! My other best friend, Claire, is the new girl at school. Both Billy and Claire know about my amazing gift, but they have pinky-sworn to secrecy.

Together, we zip around the neighborhood on our scooters, seeking out adventure. But with my abilities, adventure usually finds us first!

Okay, so you got all that? Good.

Now take a deep breath, relax your eyes, and clear your mind. My future awaits...

CHAPTER 1

Birthday Week!

"Moonbeams!" I shouted, awakened from a Sunday morning dream.

I leaped out of bed in a flurry of star-patterned bed sheets and curly black hair. I scurried out of my room and dashed down the hall.

My parents were standing in the kitchen making breakfast. "Moonbeams in a jar!" I said.

They exchanged puzzled looks and followed me into the living room.

"Is everything all right, dear?" asked my mom.

"Of course," I said, stretching across the couch. I grabbed the remote control and waved it in the air like a magic wand. "It's my birthday week, and I'm starting it off with *Beam Dreams!*"

I flicked on the television and plopped onto the couch. My frizzy curls bounced in my face, and I blew the strands away.

"What's *Beam Dreams?*" asked my dad.

"Only my new favorite show," I replied, not looking away from the TV. "There's this pretty teenager named DeeDee, see? She has a special jar of moonbeams that her dad gave to her as a gift."

"How can she carry moonbeams in a jar?" my dad wondered aloud.

I looked at him. "She just can." *Sheesh!* Sometimes dads don't get the simplest things.

"Her father's an alien from outer space with magic powers," I explained. "He gave DeeDee the moonbeams so she can have powers, too!"

My dad nodded his head. "Interesting," he said.

"DeeDee can do lots of cool stuff," I continued. "Like, one time, she turned invisible, and another time, she was flying around her room like this…"

I leaped off the couch with outstretched arms.

Just then, *Beam Dreams* started, and I returned to my spot on the couch. I sang along to the theme song while waving the remote control like a musical conductor.

Then I said, "Sometimes I feel like *I'm* from another planet."

"What do you mean, honey?" Mom asked.

"Well, I wish I was pretty and popular like DeeDee," I told my parents.

I pointed to the TV. On the screen, DeeDee sat at her bedroom vanity getting ready for school. While she brushed her hair, the golden locks glinted under the lights around the mirror.

"Her hair is so shiny and blonde," I explained. "Mine looks like an electrified squid." I tugged on a clump of curls in an effort to straighten them. When they sprang back to my head, I sighed.

"Aw, honey, your hair is beautiful," said my dad. "It looks just like mine!"

My dad has a head full of curly, bushy black hair and a bristly mustache.

He leaned over and gave me a kiss on the cheek. The hair on his upper lip tickled, but I tried not to smile. "Daaaad," I groaned. "I don't want to look like you. I want to look like DeeDee!"

"Your loss," he said, returning to the kitchen.

Mom took my hand and sat down on the couch. She smiled and gently stroked my hair. "Your hair is just one of the many different parts that make you special," she said.

"I know, Mom," I replied. "But the kids at school make fun of it. And, if they knew about my *gifts*, they would tease me even more. I wish I was a teenager like DeeDee. Teens don't have any problems at all."

"My darling, you have no idea," Mom said, chuckling. "I know you're in a rush to grow up, but trust me. You need to be happy with who you are first. Then everything else will fall into place."

I squeezed her hand. "You're right, Mom. It's just that, well, my birthday is in seven days. I'm going to be ten. That's a double digit. A big deal. I want my birthday party to be special."

"It will be," said my mom. "Grandma says she has a *very* special birthday surprise for you."

"Really?" I said. I couldn't wait to visit her.

Then Dad shouted from the kitchen. "What do you want on your French toast?"

"Blueberries, please," I replied. "But can we eat after *Beam Dreams*? It's almost over."

"Yes, dear," Mom said. "May I watch, too?"

"Sure!" I said, laying my head onto her lap.

On the TV, DeeDee's mom was painting the hallway. She had set up a ladder with a paint bucket on top of it. When DeeDee opened the door, she knocked the bucket off the ladder.

Before the can of paint could spill, DeeDee tapped her index fingers together. They sparked with electricity, and the bucket froze in midair until DeeDee carefully placed it on the floor. DeeDee's mother was happy, and the show ended.

"Yay!" I cheered. "DeeDee does it again."

"Sheesh," Dad yelled from the kitchen. "All this excitement made me hungry. Now let's eat."

Suddenly, my ears perked up, and my body tingled. This usually happened when I was getting a vision or feeling. I closed my eyes, tilted my head, and said, "Somebody's at the door..."

And then, the doorbell rang.

CHAPTER 2

Blast Off!

My dad walked over to the front door and peeked through the peephole. He couldn't see anyone. "Who is it?" he asked.

"It's Billy," I called from the living room.

"It's Billy," echoed a voice from the other side of the door.

Billy Katsikis lives in the apartment above ours with his parents and his little sister. He has round chipmunk cheeks and messy black hair.

"Good morning, everybody!" Billy cried.

He looked my dad up and down and said, "You're making French toast, aren't you?"

Dad smiled. "Why, yes, young man. How did you guess? Are you psychic, like our daughter?"

"No," Billy said, tapping his nose. "I could smell it from upstairs. I thought I'd come by and help finish any leftovers."

He rubbed his tummy. It was pushed against his dinosaur pajamas. The buttons looked ready to burst.

I hopped up from the couch and ran over to him. "Since we met you, we haven't had leftovers," I said.

"Your parents know you're here?" asked Mom.

"Yes, Mrs. Ball," answered Billy. "We already ate, but I still have room for more!"

After breakfast, Billy and I changed out of our pajamas and met at the stairs to the top floor of our building. We were going out onto the roof to play. As always, I had packed a satchel with everything we would need for the day's adventure.

"My birthday is next week, you know?" I said.

"Oh, yes," Billy replied. "And last week, your birthday was in two weeks. You made sure not to let me forget. And then, I got your party invitation in the mail a few days later. You know, you could've just handed it to me in person."

What a smart aleck. "If you want to throw a proper party," I said, "you need to send out handmade invitations by mail. Then you need to decorate and plan lots of fun games with prizes."

He smiled until his cheeks scrunched his eyes. "What about food? There better be food."

"You're driving me crazy," I told him. "Do you know how big this is? I'm going to be TEN!"

Billy replied, "You're going to be an old lady." He laughed and pushed the door open. A gust of wind blasted into the building. "Careful the wind doesn't blow you away, Granny."

I ignored him and tied a long colorful scarf over my head. I should've tied it over his mouth!

The roof area had a weatherproof table with an umbrella in the center and some chairs.

"Let's build the spaceship," Billy said.

Each of us grabbed two patio chairs and placed them a few feet apart from one another. I pulled out an old quilt from my bag.

"Ready?" I called out to Billy. "Catch!"

I tossed one end of the quilt to him, and he draped it over the two chairs.

"Mission accomplished," Billy announced. Then he bowed like a gentleman. "After you."

"Why, thank you," I said, crawling inside.

When Billy entered, I whispered, "What's on the top-secret agenda for today, Agent Katsikis?"

"Race to outer space, Agent Ball," Billy said.

We emptied out the contents of our bags. Billy brought his Galaxy Guard action figures.

I, on the other hand, brought my deluxe picture books of outer space. One of them had pop-ups of each planet. How cool is that? I also brought my model rocket that glows in the dark.

"Billy, which planet is your favorite?" I asked.

"That's easy," Billy replied. "Jupiter! It's the biggest one. And it has sixteen moons."

"That's cool," I said. But it wasn't as cool as my favorite planet. "Mine's Saturn!" I exclaimed.

I turned to the Saturn page in my pop-up book. "I like it because it wears a giant ring. See? It's the most stylish of all the planets," I said, laughing.

Billy laughed too. "Yes, very fashionable."

"It's called accessorizing," I said. Then I gasped. "Oh, that reminds me."

I rummaged through my bag, looking for all my bright-colored bracelets.

"I can't very well go into outer space without my Gauntlets of Gravity," I explained, slipping a stack of them onto each wrist.

"Of course not," Billy agreed. "Let's go!"

"Today we're going to some very glamorous galaxies," I said, propping up the books. They became the backdrop for our spaceship.

"Keep an eye out for trouble," Billy said. He pretended to steer the ship toward the Milky Way.

"Uh-oh," I shouted. "The rocket ship is on a collision course with an asteroid."

"Mayday! Mayday! Abort! Abort!" Billy cried.

I laughed and tipped backward onto the ground, yelling, "Ka-boom!"

Suddenly, my eyes closed and my body shook.

"Are you okay?" Billy asked.

I snapped out of my trance and opened my eyes. "I had a vision," I said.

"What was it? What did you see?" Billy asked.

"Cannot predict now," I replied, dazed. "But I have a bad feeling in the pit of my stomach."

Billy said, "Maybe you should have let me finish that last piece of your French toast. It's probably not agreeing with you."

"The vision was something about my party, but it was too hazy," I said. I closed my eyes and tried to bring the vision back, but it was no use.

"Well, maybe we should head inside anyway," suggested Billy. "I'm getting hungry...again."

We packed up our belongings and went downstairs.

"I'll see you later," I said.

"Yup," replied Billy, walking into his apartment. "See ya!"

As the door shut, shivers went up and down my spine like prickly little centipedes were crawling on it. "Uh-oh," I said to myself. "Something big is going to happen...and the outlook is not so good."

CHAPTER 3

Spacing Out

That night, I had the weirdest dream.

I wore a fabulous glittering silver spacesuit and climbed into a silver rocket ship. (That's not the weird part.)

"Three, two, one, blast off!" said a computer voice. The shuttle streaked through the atmosphere, and a red planet came into view.

That must be Mars, I thought. *It's exactly how it looks in my book!*

Once the space ship landed, I got off and walked around the rocky terrain. I could feel the tiny pebbles crunching under my sparkly boots.

Suddenly, Martians appeared everywhere. I was surrounded!

Is this what they look like? I wondered.

They were tall and thin, with green skin and pointy spikes sticking out of their heads. Slowly, they shuffled toward me. Some were wearing chains on their wrists, others on their legs.

"This is not the way to go," the Martians chanted together. "This is not the way to go."

The aliens advanced. I tried to push past them, but I couldn't. They started to smother me. I couldn't breathe. Finally, I let out an ear-piercing scream.

"AAAAIEEEEE!"

I sprang up in bed awake. The sun was out, and I was in the safety of my room. The Martians were gone.

Mom and Dad appeared in the doorway.

"Krystal, honey, what happened?" my mom asked.

I took a deep breath to calm myself, and said, "I was on Mars, and there were these scary Martians all around me, and they were yelling and trying to grab me and..."

"It's all right, sweetheart. It's over now," Mom said soothingly. She hugged me. "The Martians can't get you."

"I love you, Mom," I whispered back. "Thanks."

My father came over and kissed me on the forehead. He said, "Do you know where we're going today?"

I answered, "Yes! We're going to Grandma's house, of course. How could I forget."

Overjoyed, I leaped out of bed as the memory of my nightmare faded away. Then I shooed my parents out of the room so I could start getting ready for the day.

Once I was alone, I turned to Stanley, my stuffed stegosaurus. He was blue and soft with a long neck and a longer tail.

"Going to Grandma's house is always a special occasion," I said to him. "She's one of the few people that understand me."

For those of you who don't know, Grandma is special, like me. She has the gift of sight and other amazing abilities. Grandma helps and guides me whenever I feel lonely.

I opened my closet and stared at my clothes.

"What dazzling duds shall I wear?" I asked Stanley. Then it came to me. "Let's start at the top and work our way down."

I pulled out a box full of scarves. When I turned it upside down, a rainbow of colorful patterned fabrics swirled around my feet and fell to the floor. "Aha! This bright pink one with gold fringe will do," I said.

I smoothed down my unruly curls and wrapped the scarf around them. "Why don't we tie the ends at the top so we get a nice fancy bow?" I asked Stanley. The stegosaurus silently agreed.

I skipped over to the dresser and pulled open the drawer with my favorite shirts. On the top of the pile was a purple T-shirt. In its center was a gold star studded with plastic beads.

Lifting it out of the drawer, I exclaimed, "A star for a star!"

I put it on and decided to wear a long purple skirt that matched my shirt. But then I glanced at myself in the mirror.

"Hmm," I said. "Too much purple? I want to look great, not grape!"

I scratched my head until a brilliant idea popped in.

Once it did, I ran over to my scarves and picked a bright yellow one with white stripes. I tied it around my waist and let the ends dangle on one side. I had created a sensational sash.

"Much better! And now for the finishing touches," I said.

I opened my jewelry box. It was a present from Grandma on my last birthday. Inside was a little dancing ballerina. It twirled to the sweet tinkling sounds of music.

I picked out some costume jewelry that was also a gift from Grandma—a pair of gold hoop earrings and a chunky gold bracelet.

"*Voilà!*" I announced. "Am I a fashionable fortune-teller, or what?"

I did a full turn in the mirror and headed out.

Mom and Dad were waiting in the living room

when I made my grand entrance.

"Oh my, don't you look stunning!" said my mom.

"As lovely as Helen of Sparta," Dad added with a smile.

I blushed, and replied, "Thank you."

Just so you know, Helen of Sparta was the most beautiful woman in all of ancient Greece. And when she was kidnapped, her husband, King Menelaus, launched a thousand ships to bring her back home!

My dad taught me that. He likes to teach me about history and mythology. Mythology is a lot like the fairy tales I read in storybooks and the cartoons I watch on TV.

Anyway, once my parents and I were all bundled up and ready to go, we left our building. To get to Grandma's apartment, we needed to take the subway into Manhattan.

As we walked up the stairs to the elevated platform, I began to feel that tingling sensation. It was very similar to the one from the day before.

Seconds later, the train arrived. As it passed us, slowly grinding to a halt, I had a revelation.

The glinting steel of the train cars and the flickering lights reminded me of the rocket ship from my dream. The sliding doors opened, and I hesitated.

"What's the matter, dear?" my mother asked.

"Uh, nothing, Mom," I said. "I think we're about to discover what my dream was all about... so ask again later."

And with that, we climbed aboard.

CHAPTER 4

Strange Trip

As the train rattled along the tracks, I sat up in my seat to look out the window. I liked watching the buildings pass by.

"Dad," I asked. "Why is it called Queens? I don't see any castles."

My dad chuckled. "That's a good question, sweetie," he said. "I came here looking for the same thing. And when I met your mother, I knew she was going to be *my* queen forever."

Mom smiled and rolled her eyes. Dad could be a real joker sometimes.

"The truth is," Mom explained, "that Queens gets its name from Queen Catherine of Braganza. She was the wife of King Charles the Second of England."

Dad's mouth dropped open. He was pleasantly surprised with his wife.

"Yes, my dear, sometimes I pay attention to your history lessons, too," Mom told him.

Once we arrived and walked out into the city, I was super excited. "Don't you just love being here?" I asked my parents. "All the people and the lights and the buildings."

I find skyscrapers to be totally amazing.

The shorter buildings had huge billboards on top of them. They were lit up like movie screens.

My favorites were the billboards that had toys and candy on them. They were so colorful.

On every street corner, vendors had set up carts selling salty pretzels or sweet smelling treats. People hurried up and down the sidewalks. Manhattan is always buzzing with activity.

Daddy said we were only a few blocks away from Grandma's apartment building. "Right this way," he pointed. "We'll cut through 52nd Street and pass the Roseland Ballroom."

As he led us up the street, the concert hall came into view.

It had a big, lit-up sign that read: ARMY OF ARES TONIGHT ONLY!

Suddenly, my body began to tingle again, like I was getting goose bumps. I tugged on my father's sleeve. "This is not the way to go," I said. "Look!"

I pointed to the long line of people standing outside the entrance. It snaked all the way down the block and around the corner.

Mom noticed the way they were dressed. They had on ripped shirts, tight pants, and leather jackets with lots of zippers.

Their hair was dyed bright neon colors. Some only had a strip of hair down the center, spiked up into something Dad called a Mohawk.

Everyone was covered in tattoos.

"I'm assuming Army of Ares is a punk band," Mom stated.

I looked at them more closely, and yelled, "The Martians from my dream!"

As a group of punks walked by, I hid behind Dad. They looked pretty scary up close.

One of them looked over and smiled.

"Nice outfit, kid," she said to me. *Hmm, maybe they aren't so bad after all,* I thought.

Daddy was rubbing his chin. He usually did that when he was thinking.

"Interesting," he said. "Ares was the ancient Greek god of war. The Romans called him Mars. Did you know our planets are all named after Roman gods?"

"Mars is where I went in my dream," I said. "I saw Martians that looked like these people, and then it got scary."

"Well, that's that," said my mother. "If Krystal says this is not the way to go, we'll go around the block."

And so, we immediately changed course right when a large bus pulled up to the side door of the Roseland. It had the band's name spray painted on the side and filled the tiny street.

The punks standing in line cheered. They snapped pictures with their phones and cameras. The flashes lit up the alley like a strobe light. The fans ran up to the vehicle, scrambling over each other to meet the members of Army of Ares.

"Wow, cool!" Dad said, looking over his shoulder. "I remember those days."

"What do you mean?" I asked.

"I listened to punk music when I was a teenager," Dad said. "But I did not dress like that."

"That was a hundred years ago," Mom said.

"Har, har!" Dad replied. "For you, it was only ninety-eight."

"Okay, you guys, be nice," I said jokingly. Sometimes I think I'm the grown-up in the family. And, after my birthday this weekend, I was going to be one year closer.

Then I saw it. "Hey, there's Grandma's apartment building!"

Grandma's apartment building was brand new with glass doors and a large lobby. Joe, the nice doorman, greeted us. He was wearing a black uniform with gold buttons on the jacket.

There was a large bouquet of flowers in a fancy pot near the front desk. I walked over to smell them. They were gardenias.

"Gardenias are my favorite flowers," I told the young lady at the front desk.

"They're your grandmother's favorite, too," she replied. Her name tag read Mary-Kate. She knew that we came to visit Grandma. "I'll call up and tell her you're here."

Walking around the desk, Mary-Kate picked a gardenia from the vase and slipped the stem into my hair.

"You look just like your grandma," she said.

"Thank you," I replied.

It made me feel good to hear someone else say it. Maybe I was pretty after all. I looked at my reflection in one of the lobby's many mirrors. I was beaming, smiling from ear to ear.

Then Mom, Dad, and I took the elevator up to the eleventh floor.

We smelled the delicious and spicy aromas of a Grandma's meal. The smell grew stronger as we approached the apartment.

Before Dad could knock, the door swung open. Grandma stood in the doorway with her arms outstretched. She looked gorgeous. Strands of curly white hair were pulled up into a scarf tied around her head. A sash hung from her waist, covering her skirt. A fresh gardenia rested atop her ear. She *did* look just like me!

"Welcome, my darlings," Grandma said. "Lovely to see you!"

I ran over to hug her, and she kissed me on both cheeks.

"Hello, Mother," Dad said. "Sorry we're late."

"We would have been here sooner," Mom added. "But—"

"That rock-and-roll riffraff put you out of your way," Grandma replied, tapping her temple with her finger. "I know all about it. Not to worry."

Then she looked at me with a twinkle in her eye and winked.

CHAPTER 5

Grandma's House

Grandma guided us through her home. We put our coats in the closet and went straight to the kitchen. The table was set for four, with two candles burning brightly.

"Oh, this looks wonderful," said Mom, admiring the place settings.

"It smells wonderful, too," added Dad.

Grandma smiled wide with pride. "Sit down," she said. "I hope you brought your appetites."

"We sure did," I told her.

Nothing is better than Grandma's cooking, I can tell you that for sure.

Grandma put on her oven mitts and opened the oven. A smell of lemon and oregano filled the kitchen. She pulled out a large, deep pan.

"I've prepared lemon chicken in mushroom sauce with baked potatoes," she said. "There is also steamed broccoli lightly seasoned with garlic and olive oil."

"Mmm," we all said together.

"*Bon appetit*, everybody," Grandma said.

After dinner, my parents offered to clear the table and wash the dishes. "What an excellent idea," Grandma said. "Krystal, why don't you join me in the study."

"Yay!" I cheered.

Of all the rooms in Grandma's home, the study is my favorite. It's where she keeps all her most prized possessions. There are souvenirs and keepsakes from around the world.

Grandpa was a sailor who met Grandma when he was visiting a port many years ago. She was a fortune-teller in a traveling circus. They fell in love and sailed away together. Can you imagine?

As the years passed, Grandma and Grandpa worked at carnivals, wandered with gypsy camps, and even hunted for lost ancient treasures. The rest is history.

Instead of a door, the study had a beaded curtain. I loved passing my fingers over the smooth, colorful beads. I also liked that they make a clacking sound as they fell back into place.

I looked around the room and said, "Grandma, you've redecorated!"

"Well, of course I did, my child," Grandma replied. "I don't like keeping things the same old way. Variety is the spice of life."

Her framed circus posters were no longer above the desk. A large illustrated map replaced them. "What's that?" I asked, pointing to it.

"That's a map of the Seven Ancient Wonders of the World," Grandma answered. "One of them is the great pyramid at Giza in Egypt."

"Cool," I replied. "Sounds wonderful."

I walked over to an end table near the window with a very pretty wooden box.

"Ooh, Grandma! I've never seen this before," I said, tracing my finger delicately over the designs on the top. "It's beautiful."

"Yes, it is. Hand-carved, too. We got it in Egypt," Grandma said and smiled.

She stared off into the distance. "Another gift from Grandpa. He sure knew how to spoil a girl."

Grandma picked up the box and walked over to the love seat under the window. She invited me to sit next to her.

"Your grandfather and I were visiting Egypt in hopes of discovering the secrets of the pharaohs. Do you know what pharaohs are?" she asked.

"Yes," I answered. "Daddy has been teaching me about ancient Egypt. Pharaohs were kings."

"Correct, my dear," said Grandma. Then she continued, "Pharaohs also believed that they had divine power. They believed they were direct relatives of their gods."

"My favorite Egyptian goddess is Bastet," I said excitedly. "She has the body of a woman and the head of a cat. How cool is that?"

Grandma laughed and clasped my hands in hers. "Hmm. Your heart is clouded by sadness," she said. "What's troubling you?"

"It's my birthday party," I said. "I'm afraid it'll be a disaster and no one will come to it because everyone thinks I'm weird."

"Preposterous!" Grandma said. "Your friends and family love you. Why would they not come to your party? And why would they say you're weird? What makes you think otherwise?"

"It's my gift, Grandma," I replied. "It gives me scary dreams and feelings. I try to keep it a secret, but sometimes I can't. How do you handle it?"

"My darling!" Grandma said and hugged me. "It takes time and practice. We need guidance as much as the people without the gift of sight."

"Really?" I asked.

"Yes, and that's why we help our own," she explained. "My grandmother helped me the same way I'm helping you."

I started to feel a little better. It was nice to be reminded that I'm not alone.

"Cheer up, child," Grandma said, touching my cheek. "It will turn out all right in the end."

I looked up at Grandma. "How do you know?" I asked.

She smiled and opened the box. There was a stack of cards inside. They were frayed at the corners and turned yellow from being so old. Each one had an interesting illustration on it.

"Do you know what these are?" Grandma asked, fanning them out.

I shook my head no.

"These are called tarot cards," said Grandma.

"Many believe these cards date back to Thoth," she added, "the ancient Egyptian god of wisdom."

"What do they do?" I asked.

"Well, they help you think, and they help you learn. They do not tell you the future, but they will put you on your path. It's up to you to make the right choices when the time comes."

Whoa, I thought to myself. *Can a deck of cards really do that?*

"Would you like me to do a reading?" Grandma asked.

"All signs point to yes!" I answered.

Grandma shuffled the cards and took a deep breath. "Now close your eyes, dear," she said, "and tell me what you see..."

CHAPTER 6

In the Cards

I was about to get my first tarot card reading, and I wondered what the cards were going to show. Suddenly, the silence was broken by the rattle of door beads. Grandma and I both gasped.

My father popped his head into the study. "Would either of you like a cup of tea?" he asked.

"Daaad!" I cried. "You scared us."

"Wait, you mean, you didn't see me coming, Mother?" he teased.

"I was focusing on the cards, dear," Grandma said sternly. "And yes, we'll have two cups of green tea. Decaf, please."

She turned to me as soon as Dad left. That same twinkle was in her eye as before. "Your father thinks he's a comedian like Grandpa, but I don't have the heart to tell him it's not true."

I giggled a little bit.

"Now, where were we?" Grandma said as she reshuffled the cards. "Ah, yes, close your eyes, darling, and tell me what you see."

I shut my eyes and relaxed my mind. I tilted my head as a vision started to appear. It was a little murky, but it soon cleared.

"Water," I said.

"Excellent," Grandma replied. She had already turned over a card. Its image was facing up.

I looked at it. There was a picture of an angel with yellow hair and red wings wearing a long white robe. In its hands were two golden goblets. The angel was pouring water from one goblet into the other. It was standing near a lake. Underneath the image was a word: TEMPERANCE.

"Tem...per...ance," I said, sounding out the word. "What does that mean, Grandma?"

"The word means moderation, Krystal, but in the case of the card it stands for balance and harmony in life."

"Like, both good and bad?" I asked.

"Yes. In order to appreciate and enjoy the positive things in life, we must also experience the negative," Grandma explained.

She flipped over a second card and placed it next to the first. The card showed a circle in the center. It was marked with symbols or letters.

Beneath it were the words WHEEL OF FORTUNE.

"Hmm," Grandma said. "This card usually means sudden change or new developments." Then she smiled when she saw my face. "Don't worry, my child. It also means surprises."

Grandma pulled one last card. "Ah, of course," she said. "The Sun."

The card she placed on the table had a big yellow sun with a face on it. The sun's rays pointed in many different directions.

"This card symbolizes renewed energy, brilliance, and joy," Grandma explained.

"Ooh," I said. "I like the sound of that."

"My darling," said Grandma, kissing me on the forehead, "your radiance and power will always bring happiness. Do not ever forget that."

*** *

After we drank our tea, my parents and I prepared to leave. "Goodnight, Grandma," I said, hugging her goodbye.

Outside, we walked in the cold night air back to the metro stop. We passed the Roseland Ballroom where the concert was in full swing. The muffled music pounded through the outer wall. It sounded like cannons firing.

Dad smiled, and said, "Sounds like the Army of Ares is off to war!"

After the subway arrived, we were on our way back to Queens. During the ride, I had gotten so sleepy that I dozed off in Mom's arms.

When we got home, she carried me to my bedroom. "Honey, you have to put on your pajamas," Mom whispered.

While I was getting in bed, I mumbled, "Water. Water everywhere."

"What was that, sweetheart?" Mom asked. "You want some water?"

I pulled the bedsheets over my head.

"Hmm. Guess not," my mother said, shrugging her shoulders. She turned off the lamp, leaving only the Saturn-shaped night-light aglow.

Then I was fast asleep.

That night, I found myself on the deck of a large pirate ship. The sails were at full mast, and the crew bustled around me. It was sunny and warm, and the sea was a crystal clear blue.

The captain of the ship stood at the wheel, yelling commands at the men. She was wearing a feathered hat and a long red coat. There was a sword in a scabbard on her belt, and its gold hilt was glinting in the sunlight. Her long hair draped over her shoulders like a black waterfall.

Gosh, she's beautiful! I thought. *And not at all like the pirate captains I've seen in storybooks. She's even got both her hands.*

Suddenly, the ship lurched forward. We lost our balance and fell to the floor.

"Avast!" cried the captain. "To the fray!"

I had no idea what was going on. The crew prepared to fire the cannons.

The captain drew her sword. She looked at me and exclaimed, "Get down below, child. The Kraken is upon us!"

Running for cover, I asked, "What's a Kraken?" But no one answered.

Splash! Crash!

An enormous tentacle came up from the water.

"Uh, I guess, *that's* a Kraken," I said. "Or at least, part of it!"

As the creature crashed onto the deck, men scattered and wooden planks broke into pieces. I saw the sea monster's slimy suction cups scrape along the deck, leaving a trail of slippery ooze. Then another tentacle lifted high into the air. It was grasping the captain.

"Shiver me timbers!" she shouted. "I shall not be shark bait!"

With that, the captain sliced her sword through the tentacle.

The Kraken howled in pain and disappeared into the depths of the sea, causing a tidal wave. Saltwater splashed all over us. When the ship hit the shore, I crawled onto the dry sand.

"Aye, mateys," yelled the captain. She came out of the water, picked seaweed off her sopping coat, and shouted triumphantly, "We lived to tell another tale!"

There was a cheer of joy from the crew.

I splayed out on the sand like a starfish. It was nice to feel the rays of the sun warming my face. I closed my eyes and thought, *Phew, time to get some rest after such an amazing adventure.*

And then, the alarm clock rang.

CHAPTER 7

Bestie!

Rinnnnng! Rinnnnng!

Rubbing the sleep from my eyes, I shut off the alarm clock.

"Krystal, honey, breakfast is ready," yelled a voice from outside my door.

Frazzled, I pulled off my covers and headed for the kitchen. It was Monday. Can I tell you how much I dislike Mondays? What an annoying way to end a perfectly wonderful weekend.

The truth is that I really like school. It's not so bad. I just prefer that there would be less of it during the week.

I padded down the hall, my curls bouncing on top of my head.

"I'm coming, I'm coming," I cried, and when I entered the kitchen, I announced, "I'm here!"

"Good morning, sunshine," Mom said. "Your cereal is on the table."

"Mom, do you want to hear about my dream?" I asked, shoveling a spoonful into my mouth.

"Not now, dear," she said. "We're running late. You can tell me on the way."

After breakfast, I went to my bedroom to get dressed.

"Hmm, my dream has inspired me to go with an ocean-themed outfit, Stanley," I said.

Pulling a shimmery green pair of pants out of the dresser, I hopped on the bed to put them on.

"Don't these look just like the glittering scales of a mermaid's tail?" I asked my silent friend.

I slipped both feet into the pants at the same time, kicking as if I were swimming under water. I paired the pants with a light blue top. It had a

sequined goldfish on the front. I just love goldfish. They're so cute!

Then I topped it all off with a bright orange scarf and a coral necklace.

"Time to go, honey," Mom yelled from the door.

"Ahoy, matey," I responded.

She chuckled. "What are you talking about?"

"I had a dream that I was on a pirate ship," I said. I told her all about it as we walked to school. "When I was with Grandma, the tarot cards showed water. Then I saw it in my dream. It must be a sign of something in the future."

"Well, I know what's happening this Sunday," Mom said.

"It's my birthday!" I squealed and jumped up and down. "Happy birthday to me, happy birthday to me," I sang. "You know, Mom, I'm going to be a double digit. How grown-up is that?"

"It sure is," replied my mother. "Remember, we're getting the decorations after school today. One of your first grown-up responsibilities is to help me set up."

"I can't wait. The apartment will look so… *fabulous!*" I exclaimed.

As we arrived at the schoolyard, Mom kissed me on the forehead and said goodbye.

I ran up the steps into the building. Waiting there was my other best friend, Claire.

Claire Voyance had moved to Queens at the beginning of the school year. She was the new girl in class, but we hit it off immediately.

Claire has curly hair like me, but it somehow looks *way* better on her. She also wears really cute clothes, which, of course, I like.

After a few months, I shared my biggest secret with her. I tried to explain my gifts and abilities as best I could. It was nice to have a friend that I could share this stuff with. Billy's okay, but sometimes he can be so immature.

Anyway, Claire didn't breathe a word. She thought it was pretty neat to have a best friend with special powers. She acts like I'm a superhero.

"Hi, Claire!" I shouted.

"Hi, Krystal!" Claire shouted back. She ran over and grabbed me by the wrist.

Suddenly, I felt the tingles and energy wash over my body. It was warm and fuzzy, like a happy feeling. I shut my eyes and caught a glimpse of something red and pink.

"It's about time you got here," Claire cried, distracting me. "We have soooo much to talk about."

We ran down the hall to Miss Callisto's fourth grade classroom.

"Good morning, girls," Miss Callisto said as we entered the room.

"Good morning, Miss Callisto," we replied at the same time.

As the teacher prepared our lesson, Claire and I took our assigned seats. Luckily, our desks are right next to each other.

"I got your birthday invitation in the mail," Claire whispered.

Like I mentioned earlier, I created the invitations to my birthday all by myself. I used construction paper, markers, a gel pen, and lots and lots of glitter. Okay, so my mom helped me mail them out, but still, it's all very impressive to do on your own.

Claire unloaded her backpack onto the desk. Her books flapped open and clattered against the hard surface. The pink card I sent her fluttered out last.

I looked down and gasped.

Then I whispered into Claire's ear, "You like Billy Katsikis?"

She bolted upright in her seat and turned as red as her hair.

"What? How do you know?" Claire asked. Then she lowered her voice. "Did you read my mind?"

I laughed. "No, I can't do that," I said.

I pointed to the notebook that dropped out of Claire's bag. It had fallen open to a blank page. There, on the bottom with a big red heart doodled around it was Billy's name.

"It's kind of obvious," I said.

"Ohmygosh!" Claire cried.

In a flash, she ripped the page out of her notebook and crumpled it up. Then she shoved it into her bag and sat on it so no one else could see.

"Is everything all right, Claire?" Miss Callisto asked her.

"Just peachy!" she replied.

Then she turned to me and said, "I guess we both have our secrets, huh?"

"Don't worry, bestie," I said, putting a hand on her shoulder. "Your secret is safe with me."

CHAPTER 8

My Worst Nightmare

Finally, the school day ended. Claire and I skipped out of the classroom.

"I'm so excited about your birthday party," Claire squealed. She looked over to see Billy and the other boys from our class horsing around on the front lawn. "Has Billy responded yet? Is he going to be there?"

"He better be there," I said. "We live together."

"Oooh," Claire said, making kissy-face noises.

"Stop that," I said. "I mean we live in the same building. I'm just worried that no one else will be there and that it will be a disaster."

"What are you talking about?" Claire said. "Everyone in the class is super excited about your birthday party."

"Really?" I said. I was pleasantly surprised. Before I could respond, Claire interrupted me.

"Boy, for someone who can read minds, you don't know how much your friends like you."

I smiled wide, and yelled, "I can't read minds, Claire!"

Then we heard the sound of a car horn. Mrs. Voyance signaled to Claire from her car.

"Krystal, I have to go," she said. "Promise you won't tell anyone about...you know what."

"I promise."

"Pinky promise," Claire said.

"Okay," I replied.

We interlocked our pinkies, forming the sacred bond of the pinkie promise. Then Claire waved goodbye and went home.

I saw Mom walking up the sidewalk, and I ran up to her.

"How was school, honey?" she asked.

"Fine," I said. "Today we learned about fractions, but I also learned something about my friend, Claire."

"Really? What?" Mom asked.

"Oops," I said, remembering the pinkie promise. "I can't tell you. It's a secret."

"In that case, forget I asked," Mom said. "Ready to go shopping?"

"Aw, yeah!" I said.

The party supply store was right near the school. Inside, each aisle was decorated with a specific theme. My favorite was always the carnival and circus aisle.

"Mom, look," I cried, pointing to a row of feathered masks. "These are amazing."

I tried one on while Mom filled her basket with streamers and garlands.

A woman with an overstuffed shopping cart pushed past in a hurry. She had an oversized hairdo piled high atop her head and an oversized bag hanging from her shoulder.

"Excuse me," she said, rushing to the register.

Excuse you! I thought. I dove out of her way but was grazed by the shoulder bag. I managed to glean a vision from it.

I closed my eyes and tilted my head. The vision came into focus. Then I walked over to the teenaged stock boy straightening the shelves.

"Hi, mister," I said, tugging on his apron. "You may want to clean up the mess in the next aisle."

The stock boy walked over to where I was pointing. He looked down the aisle. All he saw was the rude woman with the overstuffed cart. She was barreling past a tall pyramid display of cone-shaped party hats.

The teenager looked confused. "Uh, I don't see any—" he began.

Before he could finish his sentence, the woman's bag sideswiped the pyramid display. It teetered back and forth a few times before toppling over. Whoosh!

The woman yelped as she was covered in an avalanche of paper hats. The stock boy ran over as fast as he could.

"My hair!" the woman shrieked.

The pointy ends of some party hats were stuck inside her beehive.

"My art," the teenager yelled, picking up the scattered items. "Now I have to create the display all over again."

I covered my mouth to stop laughing out loud and went to help Mom finish shopping.

***

When Mom paid for the supplies, we headed home. Billy was sitting on the front steps of our building. I sprinted toward him.

"Hey, Billy," I said. "Look what I got."

I held up a bag full of party supplies. Billy didn't look up. In fact, he was hiding his face. His eyes were red.

"What's the matter?" I asked.

"Bad news," Billy said glumly.

He nodded toward a white van parked on the street. It said PAULY'S PLUMBING on its side.

"I flooded the bathroom," Billy said.

"Ew!" I said, holding my nose. "That's gross."

Billy smiled halfheartedly. "I wish that's what happened," he said. "I thought it would be cool to film a home movie with my digital camera."

"It was going to be an ocean adventure," he continued. "I had my pirate ship and my rubber sea creatures and everything."

The hairs on my arms stood up. *Pirate ship. Sea creatures.* "I had a dream just like that," I interrupted.

"Whoa," Billy replied. "Do you think it was a premonition?"

"Well, what happened next?" I asked.

"I turned on the water to fill the tub, right? And I had the camera in one hand, and I was splashing the ship with the other like this..."

Billy demonstrated his filmmaking technique as he spoke. "I figured that would make the attack look more realistic, which it totally did," he said. "Then I switched off the camera but forgot to turn off the water."

"Uh-oh," I said.

"Exactly," agreed Billy. "The water poured out of the tub, onto the floor, and out the front door. My parents called the plumber and the landlord. They say I caused a lot of damage. And that I'm in *big* trouble."

"I'm sorry to hear that," I replied.

"Yeah, it's a bummer," Billy said. "But that's pretty cool about your dream, though."

I stood up and said, "I have got to tell my parents what happened. You see, my dream was showing me the future."

"Okay," Billy said. "I'll catch you later."

I ran all the way up to our apartment, taking the stairs two steps at a time. The door was open.

"Mom? Dad? Where are you?" I yelled.

"We're in the living room, honey," Dad answered.

"You'll never guess what happened," I said.

When I walked into the room, I stopped dead in my tracks. I could not believe my eyes. Immediately, I started to cry.

CHAPTER 9

The Water Works

The living room looked like it had been hit by an earthquake. A big soggy chunk of ceiling had fallen on the coffee table. Its broken pieces splattered across the carpet, the sofa, and the TV.

Mom ran over to me. "It's okay, honey. We're all fine. Don't worry," she said, wiping away my tears.

"What happened?" I couldn't stop staring at the opening in the ceiling. There were metal pipes and wooden beams crisscrossing each other.

"From the looks of it, I'd say the flooding upstairs compromised the integrity of our ceiling," Dad replied.

"Huh?" I said.

"Meaning, all that water seeped through the floor and was absorbed by our ceiling like a sponge," my mother explained. "These materials aren't made to hold water, and they collapsed under the weight."

"But not to worry," Dad added. "The landlord will have it fixed in a week. Good as new."

"A week!" I shrieked. "No!"

I started sobbing again. Forget all my other worries, this was a real disaster.

"Krystal's birthday party is on Saturday, dear," Mom said.

Dad's face dropped. "Oh, I'm sure we can—"

Suddenly, There was a knock at the door. We turned to see Billy standing there.

"I'm really sorry," he said quietly.

"I hate you," I shouted, "and I never want to see you again."

I was so angry. I ran into my room and slammed the door.

A few seconds later, there was a knock. "Krystal, honey, may I come in?"

"Just leave me alone," I yelled.

"I'm your mother," she stated. "I will not just leave you alone."

She came in and sat next to me on the bed.

"The living room is ruined," I sniffed. "My party is ruined. I knew it."

"Darling, don't worry," Mom said soothingly. "We'll postpone it. That's all."

"Mother," I groaned. "I wanted to have it on the same day. If we postpone it, I'll already be ten at the party." I threw my arms in the air, adding, "What's the point, then?"

Mom smiled. "You're quite the drama queen, you know? Just like your grandmother."

Suddenly, I sat up straight. All this information came flooding back into my head.

"Grandma!" I exclaimed. "That's it! When she read the cards, she said that they would not tell me the future but put me on my path."

"What do you mean, sweetheart?" Mom asked.

I blew my nose into a tissue, and said, "Temperance, Mom. That means balance and harmony. I must experience bad things to appreciate the good ones. In my dream, the pirate ship was destroyed, but the crew lived. It was a premonition of the living room."

"I see," replied Mom. She looked confused. "But I don't think we were in any danger from a few pounds of falling plaster."

"That's not what I'm talking about," I continued. "Grandma said that I had to make the right choice when the time came. I see now that I made the wrong choice."

"You mean, yelling at Billy the way you did?"

"Yes," I said, looking at my feet. "I shouldn't have said such a mean thing. I know my birthday is a big deal to me, but my friendship with Billy is more important than a party."

"Whoa, slow down, honey," Mom said, chuckling. "It's not even Sunday, and already you're growing up right before my eyes."

I smiled and kissed her. "I love you, Mom." Then I ran out of my room to find my friend.

I went up to Billy's apartment and knocked on the door. When he opened it, I hugged him.

"Do you have the wrong address?" Billy asked.

"You're still my best friend," I said.

"Phew!" said Billy, wiping his brow. "What a relief! I'm sorry too." He invited me in. "You want something to eat? My mom made dinner." Then in a whisper, "It tastes better if you hold your nose."

I laughed. "No, thank you. I have to go home and help my parents clean."

"Yeah, me too," Billy said. "Hey, why don't I tell everyone tomorrow that I got you a new sunroof for your birthday? That way, they'll get jealous and have to bring you something much cooler."

My stomach did a flip when the truth hit me again. I said, "That's sweet, Billy, but there isn't going to be a party anymore."

CHAPTER 10

Crystal Clear

The rest of the week went by in a blur. I was so bummed. I went to school and did my homework. The landlord and his construction crew started repairing the hole in the ceiling. They had blocked off the living room and worked around the clock. In three days, they'd be finished.

On Friday, the night before my birthday, I was in bed tossing and turning. When I did fall asleep, I had another frightening dream.

I found myself in an empty and dark amusement park. The merry-go-round and the Ferris wheel stood silently like unmoving guards.

I walked past the different game booths. All of them were closed down and boarded up. Suddenly, I smelled smoke. I kept walking and saw a soft orange glow.

Soon, the glow grew brighter. Five figures came out of the darkness carrying lanterns on long metal staffs. I squinted to look at their faces.

They were clowns. Creepy-looking clowns with white faces, red noses, and colorful clothes. They were headed right for me.

I turned and ran as fast as I could. I needed to get out of there. As I sprinted toward the exit, one by one the rides magically turned on. They had a life of their own. Bright lights blinked on and off in time to carnival music.

I was a few feet from freedom when my way was blocked. Five more clowns appeared, also holding lanterns.

I turned to run the way I came, but the first clowns caught up to me. All ten stood in a circle and raised their lanterns high. Then, without warning, they smashed them on the ground.

Flames burst up, creating a circle of fire around me. I was trapped inside it! The clowns started laughing and clapping. Then their legs started to stretch. They became taller and taller just as the flames burned brighter and hotter. They towered over me like giants, laughing and clapping and singing along to the carnival music.

I didn't know which way to go. With my arms outstretched, I started spinning and spinning, looking for a way out. I spun so fast that I lifted off the ground. I kept spinning.

The wind swirled around me faster and faster until I became a tornado. Then all of a sudden…

Shoom!

The flames disappeared and the clowns blew far away. The music stopped and the lights went out. Darkness returned and I landed with a thud on the ground. Oof!

***

At nearly eleven o'clock, I awoke and found myself tangled in my sheets. I was groggy and dizzy. I had overslept, and the images from my dream were still fresh in my mind. It was finally my birthday, and yet I was less than thrilled.

As I got out of bed I heard my mother yell, "Krystal, honey, we're leaving in a few minutes."

Then Dad said, "We're all going to Cozy Bozo's, your favorite restaurant."

Cozy Bozo's was my favorite restaurant because it had a large play area with amusement park type rides, activities, video games and prizes. But then I remembered my dream and shivered. What if it was a sign that something worse was going to happen? The coincidence was too eerie to ignore.

"It was only a dream, Krystal," I told myself. "You're ten now. You're a big girl. A grown-up."

I put on the skirt and shirt I had picked out the night before. Once the finishing touches were in place, I made my grand entrance.

"Ta-da!" I announced, showing off. A red and white striped scarf covered my hair, and a string of blue pearls hung from my neck.

"What a beautiful birthday girl," said Dad.

"Happy Birthday, Krystal!" Mom said.

I thanked them as we left the apartment and headed for the restaurant.

At Cozy Bozo's, my parents and I were greeted by a hostess wearing a ringmaster's costume. She escorted us to a private party room in the back. Dad opened the door and ushered us in.

I stopped, frozen in place. The big room was dark. My body tingled and felt the same feeling from my dream. There was a smell of smoke and a yellow-orange glow coming my way.

"Mom, Dad," I pleaded, "something bad is going to happen. I just know it."

I turned to run out the door when suddenly—

"Surprise!"

The lights turned on. I whirled around to find an unbelievable sight: Grandma was standing in the center of the room holding a birthday cake.

Ten striped candles burned brightly on top.
All around her were my friends from school,
including Claire and Billy!

I was shocked. It was a surprise birthday party
just for me. I looked at my parents and shouted,
"Thank you!"

The crowd started singing "Happy Birthday".

"Oh, my stars!" I exclaimed, hopping up and down. "Thank you so much. I can't believe it. I couldn't have dreamed of a better birthday party."

"See," Grandma said, "everything turned out all right. Now close your eyes and make a wish."

I did just that and blew out the candles. And no, I won't tell you what it was, because then it won't come true.

"Okay, listen up," Mom said. "There's pizza and punch for everybody on the table. Dig in and go have fun."

Dad added, "We'll call you back when it's time for cake and presents."

My friends ran cheering to the food and games.

"Mmm...pizza," Billy yelled.

Claire and I watched him inhale his first slice as if the world was going to stop making pizza.

"Hi, Claire," he said between mouthfuls. "You better eat some before it's all gone."

Billy shoved the crust into his mouth. His cheeks puffed out like a chipmunk's.

"Want to get some punch?" he asked Claire.

She blushed and stammered, "S-s-sure."

Walking with Billy to the drinks, Claire looked over her shoulder at me. I gave her a thumbs-up.

After we tired ourselves out with the food and games, I sat in the center of the room and opened all my presents.

Claire gave me a glow-in-the-dark wall poster of all eighty-eight constellations. Billy gave me a bright pink rain jacket, which he thought was rather funny. I did too, I guess.

Finally, my dad handed me a small, square box. "Let's not forget my gift," he said.

I opened it and gasped. "Oh my gosh, is this what I think it is?"

"Of course, sweetheart," he replied. "Your very own crystal ball."

"It's perfect!" I exclaimed.

"I figured you needed a place to keep all those powers," Dad added. "You know, those *moonbeams* of yours." He winked.

"Thanks, Dad," I said, "although I don't need a crystal ball to finally see that I have great friends and family. I love you all so much."

Everyone cheered. Dad gave me a hug. I was the happiest girl in the world.

Then I put the crystal ball down on the table. I placed my hands on the smooth, cool orb and closed my eyes. My ears perked up, and I tilted my head to the side.

The room grew silent. The guests crowded a little closer.

"I'm having a vision," I said.

"Is it good?" Claire asked.

"Is it bad?" asked Billy.

"Better not tell you now," I replied. "It'll spoil the fun."

"Aw, come on!" Billy begged.

In a loud clear voice, I gave my final prediction:

"It is certain. With all of you at my side, a great adventure is always guaranteed."

Ruby Ann Phillips

Ruby Ann Phillips is the pseudonym of a *New York Times* bestselling author who lives in the Big Apple, in a neighborhood much like Krystal Ball's.

Sernur Isik

Sernur Isik lives in magical Istanbul,
Turkey. As a child, she loved drawing
fairies and unicorns, as well as
wonderful, imaginative scenes of her
home country. Since graduating from
the Fine Arts Faculty-Graphic Design of
Ataturk University, Sernur has worked
as a professional illustrator and artist
for children's books, mascot designs,
and textile brands. She likes collecting
designer toys, reading books, and
traveling the world.

Horoscopes by Krystal Ball!

Astrologists believe a diagram of the position of stars and planets on a person's birthday foretells the future. This diagram is divided into twelve groups called signs. Find your sign and Krystal's prediction for your future!

ARIES (MAR 21–APR 19)

Krystal says: "You're fun, creative, and a natural born leader. With a little focus, you'll find yourself at the head of the class!"
Lucky numbers: 2, 17, 63

TAURUS (APR 20–MAY 20)

Krystal says: "As a thoughtful, patient friend, others often turn to you for advice. Don't be afraid to listen to yourself, too!"
Lucky numbers: 5, 12, 42

GEMINI (MAY 21–JUN 21)

Krystal says: "Although you're SUPER smart, a big decision will be difficult to make. Follow your heart, and you'll be fine!"
Lucky numbers: 6, 18, 75

CANCER (JUN 22–JUL 22)

Krystal says: "You know what you like, but don't be afraid to try something new—like pineapple on pizza! It's better than it sounds."
Lucky numbers: 10, 22, 81

LEO (JUL 23–AUG 22)

Krystal says: "You've got a big heart! Make sure your smile matches it, even when times are tough."
Lucky numbers: 4, 37, 56

VIRGO (AUG 23–SEP 22)

Krystal says: "You like to plan things carefully. Don't forget to relax once in a while—especially during your favorite TV show!"
Lucky numbers: 3, 13, 23

LIBRA (SEP 23–OCT 22)

Krystal says: "You're polite and kind, but don't let people walk all over you—they'll ruin your outfit!"

Lucky numbers: 15, 88, 97

SCORPIO (OCT 23–NOV 21)

Krystal says: "Friends trust you with their secrets. Open up and trust them with some of your own."

Lucky numbers: 9, 29, 55

SAGITTARIUS (NOV 22–DEC 21)

Krystal says: "You have a gazillion friends. Pick one to give a little extra attention!"

Lucky numbers: 16, 38, 54

CAPRICORN (DEC 22–JAN 19)

Krystal says: "You work hard, but don't forget to PLAY. Or better yet, try out for a part in one instead!"

Lucky numbers: 7, 21, 77

AQUARIUS (JAN 20–FEB 18)

Krystal says: "You're creative and unique. Don't be afraid to show your style with fashion. I'm not!"

Lucky numbers: 19, 46, 92

PISCES (FEB 19–MAR 20)

Krystal says: "Sometimes following your dreams can seem like a nightmare. Don't give up on them!"

Lucky numbers: 28, 81, 99

Krystal's Fortune Game!

Krystal Ball's favorite game predicts the future 100% of the time, although it's not always 100% accurate!

What you'll need:

- A pencil or pen
- Plenty of paper
- One or more friends!

1. First, ask one of your friends for the following information:
   - Name four places in the world you want to live.
   - Name four jobs you would like to have.
   - Name four random numbers.

2. Using your pencil or pen, write down their answers in three separate lists, like this:

Paris	Doctor	3
New York	Fire Fighter	209
London	Soccer Player	15
Minneapolis	Fortune-teller	10,000

3. Next, ask your friend to choose a number between 1 and 10.

4. Then, begin counting through the items in your friend's lists. When you reach the number your friend chose, stop and cross out the item.

5. For example, if your friend chose the number 6, cross out the sixth item in the lists, like this:

Paris	Doctor	3
New York	~~Fire Fighter~~	209
London	Soccer Player	15
Minneapolis	Fortune-teller	10,000

6. Beginning where you left off, start counting again. When you reach the number your friend chose, cross out the item.

7. Continue this process, skipping the items you've already crossed out. When only one item remains in a list, circle it! You're finished when your paper looks like this:

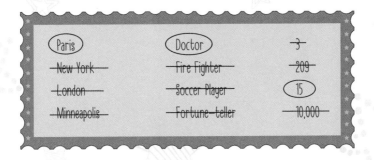

(Paris)	(Doctor)	~~3~~
~~New York~~	~~Fire Fighter~~	~~209~~
~~London~~	~~Soccer Player~~	(15)
~~Minneapolis~~	~~Fortune-teller~~	~~10,000~~

8. Finally, tell your friend their fortune: "You will live in Paris, working as a doctor, with 15 pets!"

9. Be creative! Make up new questions to ask. Then find another friend to play Krystal's Fortune Game!

See what the future holds for...

Krystal ★Ball

Read another book to find out!

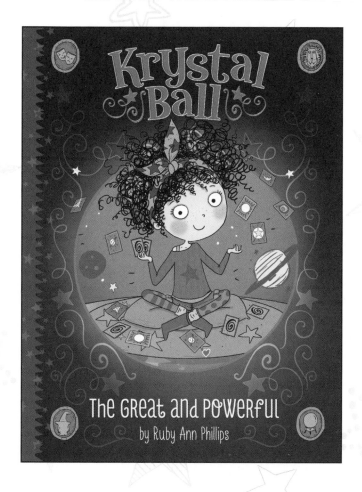

THE FUN DOESN'T STOP HERE!

Discover more at www.capstonekids.com

Videos & Contests/Games & Puzzles
Friends & Favorites/Authors & Illustrators

Find cool websites and more books like this one at www.facthound.com.

Just type in the Book ID: 9781479521784 and you are ready to go!